Reginald Parker Oliver Vine

Joanna Weaver
Illustrated by Tony Kenyon

Faith Kids® is an imprint of Cook Communications Ministries,
Colorado Springs, Colorado 80918
Cook Communications, Paris, Ontario
Kingsway Communications, Eastbourne, England

REGINALD PARKER OLIVER VINE
© 2000 by Joanna Weaver for text and Tony Kenyon for illustrations

Editor: Kathy Davis
Graphic Design: Granite Design
First printing, 2000
Printed in Singapore
04 03 02 01 00   5 4 3 2 1

Library of Congress Cataloging-in-Publication Data
Weaver, Joanna.
    Reginald Parker Oliver Vine/Joanna Weaver; illustrated by Tony Kenyon.
        p. cm. — (Attitude adjusters)
    Summary: No one wants to play with Reginald Parker Oliver Vine because
    of his constant whining and complaining, but his attitude improves after
    he prays to Jesus.
        ISBN 0-7814-3369-X
        [1. Behavior—Fiction. 2. Christian life—Fiction. 3. Stories in rhyme.]
    I. Kenyon, Tony, ill. II. Title.
    PZ8.3.W3797 Re 2000
    [E]—dc21   99-089815

This book belongs to:

_____

"Do everything without complaining or arguing . . ."
Philippians 2:14 (NIV)

Reginald Parker Oliver Vine
was such a nice boy,
except when he'd whine.

He whined in the morning,
he whined in the night.
He whined during breakfast
between every bite.

"I wanted cereal,
    the snap-crackle kind."
His mother would bring it,
    but still Reggie whined.

"It's yucky, it's icky,
oh, take it away!"
Then he grumbled and mumbled
the rest of the day.

He whined in the bathtub,
    he whined in the pool.
He whined playing baseball,
    and even at school.

"That's my ball!" he'd holler.
"Give it back," he would shout.
Then he'd scream and turn red
till he'd nearly pass out.

His teacher said, "Reggie, remember to share."
"But it's mine . . . I found it. It just isn't fair!"

Well, soon little Reggie
was left all alone.
No one would play when he'd
gripe and he'd moan.

Everyone left him;
   they just walked away.
So he played by himself for
   two weeks and one day.

To play "Mother, May I?" was
really quite hard.
It took him all recess to cross
the schoolyard.

Trying to seesaw just wasn't
the same.
He needed a playmate to make
it a game.

He tried playing catch, but got bonked on the head.
So Reggie sat down and he pouted instead.

"I feel so alone," he said with a tear.
   "Nobody does nothin' for me around here."

"I don't care," said Reggie.
"So what? Big fat deal.
Who needs them anyway . . . "

"I do!" he squealed.

Sally Jean Stuart walked up and she said,
 "Hey, little boy with the bump on your head . . ."

"I've noticed you're lonely. You really look sad.
Jesus sure helps me when I'm feeling bad.
Just pray and ask Him. He'll help you, it's true.
He loves little children like me and like you."

23

So Reginald Parker Oliver Vine knelt
    and he prayed without one single whine.
"I know I've been rude.
    I've been cranky and mean.
Forgive me, dear Jesus,
    and make my heart clean.
Help me start over and maybe I'll be
    more like You, Jesus, and less like old me."

25

What happened that day it was strange,
it was wild.
Little by little, people saw
a new child.

When Reggie ate breakfast, he smiled
    and said, "Thanks!"
He sang in the tub while he played
    with toy tanks.

He took turns at recess
	and shared baseball mitts.
He no longer grumbled,
	he stopped throwing fits.

Soon Reginald Parker Oliver Vine
    had friends by the gazillions all standing in line.

I Can Be Happy with What I Have

Ages: 4-7

Life Issue: I don't want my child to make a habit of grumbling and complaining.

Spiritual Building Block: Contentment

Learning Styles

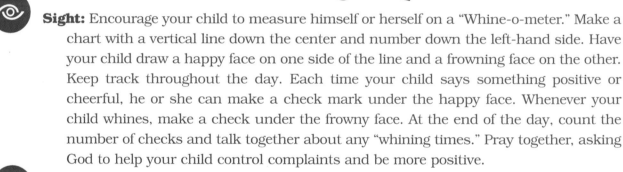

Sight: Encourage your child to measure himself or herself on a "Whine-o-meter." Make a chart with a vertical line down the center and number down the left-hand side. Have your child draw a happy face on one side of the line and a frowning face on the other. Keep track throughout the day. Each time your child says something positive or cheerful, he or she can make a check mark under the happy face. Whenever your child whines, make a check under the frowny face. At the end of the day, count the number of checks and talk together about any "whining times." Pray together, asking God to help your child control complaints and be more positive.

Sound: Challenge your child to a whining contest. See if you can top each other by whining about silly and ridiculous things. Then see who can get the other to laugh first by making up the funniest complaint. After you've had a good giggle together, talk about real whining and why it can be such a problem. Explain that we need to develop joyful hearts that see the good in life's situations. Conclude by thanking God for some good things in your world.

Touch: Play a game called "Downside, Upside." Gather some household items together and put them in a grab bag (using a pillowcase or paper bag). Items could include a piece of fruit, an old book, a spoon, a carrot, a worn-out toy, or anything that doesn't have an obvious value. In this game, your child draws an item out of the bag, as if it were a prize. He or she should tell what its "downside" is first (for example, it's broken, it's not a favorite food, it's old, and so on). Then think about what might be good about that item and tell its "upside." Point out that the item didn't change, but the way you thought about it did. Looking for the good in it made the prize seem better.